PROTECTING THE ENVIRONMENT

THE ENVIRONMENT: *OURS TO SAVE*

PROTECTING THE ENVIRONMENT

EDITED BY SHERMAN HOLLAR

Britannica Educational Publishing
IN ASSOCIATION WITH
ROSEN
EDUCATIONAL SERVICES

Published in 2012 by Britannica Educational Publishing
(a trademark of Encyclopædia Britannica, Inc.)
in association with Rosen Educational Services, LLC
29 East 21st Street, New York, NY 10010.

Distributed exclusively by Rosen Educational Services.
For a listing of additional Britannica Educational Publishing titles, call toll free (800) 237-9932.

First Edition

Britannica Educational Publishing
Michael I. Levy: Executive Editor, Encyclopædia Britannica
J.E. Luebering: Director, Core Reference Group, Encyclopædia Britannica
Adam Augustyn: Assistant Manager, Encyclopædia Britannica

Anthony L. Green: Editor, Compton's by Britannica
Michael Anderson: Senior Editor, Compton's by Britannica
Sherman Hollar: Associate Editor, Compton's by Britannica

Marilyn L. Barton: Senior Coordinator, Production Control
Steven Bosco: Director, Editorial Technologies
Lisa S. Braucher: Senior Producer and Data Editor
Yvette Charboneau: Senior Copy Editor
Kathy Nakamura: Manager, Media Acquisition

Rosen Educational Services
Jeanne Nagle: Senior Editor
Nelson Sá: Art Director
Cindy Reiman: Photography Manager
Karen Huang: Photo Researcher
Matthew Cauli: Designer, Cover Design
Introduction by Jeanne Nagle

Library of Congress Cataloging-in-Publication Data

Protecting the environment / edited by Sherman Hollar.
p. cm.—(The environment: ours to save)
"In association with Britannica Educational Publishing, Rosen Educational Services."
Includes bibliographical references and index.
ISBN 978-1-61530-503-2 (library binding)
1. Environmental protection—Juvenile literature. I. Hollar, Sherman.
TD170.15.P76 2012
333.72—dc22

2010049692

Manufactured in the United States of America

On the cover (inset): An ecologist tests stream water. *Shutterstock.com*

Front cover background, back cover, p. 2 © www.istockphoto.com/Aimin Tang; Interior background: Leaves. www.istockphoto.com/Elena Elisseeva

Contents

INTRODUCTION

Here's an interesting question: What would you be willing to do to make sure you and your family were happy and safe? Most people are likely to say they'd work hard to earn money, or defend themselves and their loved ones against any and all threats. Smart folks might also consider taking steps to protect the environment. Considering how important nature is to human survival, protecting it is pretty much the same thing as safeguarding the future of people everywhere.

Conservation is the science of making sure that nature keeps working the way it should, while at the same time taking into account the human need for natural resources. As the name indicates, conservation is about conserving, or carefully using and maintaining levels of, the resources nature provides, including water, forests (wood), soil, minerals, fossil fuels, and wildlife. This book examines

Volunteers clean rubbish from the banks of the Yamuna River in India. *Prakash Singh/AFP/Getty Images*

the conservation of these resources, detailing protection efforts past and present, as well as the consequences of not safeguarding these particular sectors of the environment.

After oxygen, water is the single most vital element for the survival of every living thing on Earth. A renewable resource, water is plentiful in many parts of the world. However, some areas are naturally arid while others experience droughts. Also, pollution can ruin bodies of water. Conservation methods such as protecting natural water sources from pollution and planting greenery to help the ground soak up rain are the best ways to make sure everyone has access to clean water for drinking, cleaning, and growing food crops.

Forests provide wood for heating and building, plus they are home to a number of unique plants and animals. Trees of the forest are a renewable resource, but it takes time for them to grow to the point where they are useful. Reducing the number of trees that are cut down and slowing down the rate at which necessary logging occurs are among the conservation efforts used to save forests.

In slang terms, soil is not considered very valuable; being "treated like dirt" would make someone feel worthless. Yet in truth, soil is one of Earth's most precious natural resources. It provides food and shelter to a number of creatures that live in it and on it. Plants and crops couldn't grow without the nutrients found in the top layer of soil. Protecting soil mainly involves keeping the life-giving top layer from being washed away in the rain or blowing away in the wind.

Deep within the soil are vital minerals and fossil fuels, including coal, oil, and natural gas. Humans are dependent on these nonrenewable resources for nutrition and construction (minerals) as well as heating and transportation (fossil fuels). But the limited supply of these resources make conservation an absolute must.

Wildlife conservation protects animals from becoming endangered or extinct. This is important because each living thing on Earth plays a role in keeping the planet alive and well. Simply by living as they are designed to live, wild animals provide what scientists call "ecological services." These include cleaning the air and water, enriching the soil, pollinating crops, reducing harmful species, and helping to keep the climate stable.

Conservation is definitely a balancing act. But in order to protect the environment—and the future of the entire planet—it is a totally worthwhile effort.

CHAPTER 1
Goals of Conservation

Conservation is the responsible stewardship, or management, of the environment, which tries to find a balance between preserving nature and the human need for products and recreation that nature provides. People vary in their opinions

A great egret wades amid cypress trees in Florida's Everglades National Park, which preserves the largest subtropical wilderness left in the United States. Roughly half of the original natural Everglades area has been destroyed, mainly for land development. National Park Service

on the levels of importance of the various components and on how much emphasis should be placed on each. Thus, some people view the primary function of conservation as a mechanism to preserve natural habitats and wildlife, whereas others view conservation as the means to assure the persistence of economically important natural resources that are of direct benefit to humans. However, most agree that a major goal of conservation today is reasonable use of Earth's natural resources in the broadest sense, which includes water, soil, wildlife, forests, minerals, and fossil fuels.

Freshwater habitats must be kept clean for drinking and recreational activities. Soils must be kept fertile, without the accumulation of toxic chemicals from pesticides or herbicides, to provide fruits and vegetables and to prevent poisoning of wildlife. Forests must be managed to provide not only lumber and pulpwood for paper products but also homes and food for native wildlife. The use of oil, coal, and minerals important for an industrial society must be carefully monitored to be certain that the supply does not dwindle too rapidly, and that natural habitats are not degraded in the process of producing and using them.

Natural resources are sometimes classified as renewable or nonrenewable. Forests, grasslands, wildlife, and soil are examples of renewable resources. They can be regenerated through natural processes, and prudent management can maintain them at steady levels. The consumption of the limited supplies of nonrenewable fossil fuels such as coal, petroleum, and natural gas, whether wasteful or not, speeds their depletion. Conservation includes measures toward reduced usage of fossil fuels. Likewise, certain nonrenewable critical ores and metals, such as iron, aluminum (bauxite), and copper, have finite supplies and controlled accessibility that sometimes call for conservation measures, such as recycling programs, to assure continued production.

Another goal of conservation is to preserve the natural beauty of a community. When land is mistreated, the countryside can become aesthetically unpleasant. Vacant lots covered with trash, bare roadsides, garbage-laden streams, and the unregulated sprawl of strip malls are considered ugly by most people. Conservation also helps to preserve areas suitable for recreation. As cities grow crowded, natural areas become more scarce. In order for people to enjoy their leisure

Ducks swim amid garbage in a polluted waterway. Refuse-clogged rivers and canals are more than just unsightly. They also pose a threat to wildlife. **Shutterstock.com**

time, they need, or can benefit greatly from, city parks, wildlife preserves, and national parks; grass and trees bordering roads and highways; and clear rivers and streams.

Natural resources are a vital part of sustaining human life. Conservation measures are designed to control, manage, and preserve them so that they can be used and appreciated to the fullest. A proper conservation program incorporates effective measures so that all natural resources are managed in the best interest of everyone.

HISTORY OF ENVIRONMENTAL ABUSES IN THE UNITED STATES

The settlement of the United States provides a dramatic example of the unsustainable depletion of resources. When the first European settlers arrived in North America, they found a continent rich in natural resources. Much of the land was covered with forests where wild animals abounded. Great herds of bison roamed the grasslands. The soil was deep and fertile. Clean lakes and streams, unpolluted with silt and chemical wastes, held a wealth of fish.

Surrounded by what seemed to be unending supplies of natural resources, and in the struggle to obtain food, clothing, and shelter, settlers cut down millions of acres of the Eastern forests. As they moved westward, they plowed up the native grasslands to plant corn (maize) and wheat. Their growing cities dumped sewage and waste material from factories and homes into the lakes and streams.

A Texas farm turned into a dust bowl during the 1930s. Overfarming lessens the natural vegetation on the land, leaving the soil unable to absorb and retain moisture. Three Lions/Hulton Archive/Getty Images

Much of the spring and summer rain in the United States falls in torrential thunderstorms, especially in the vast Missouri, Mississippi, and Ohio river basins. The farmers who settled the country were mainly

Europeans who had been used to gentle rains. The methods of tilling and planting that they brought with them and with which they were familiar were not suited to the new climate.

Further complicating matters, the land's capacity for storing water was diminished by the loss of grasses that hold the soil in place and prevent the escape of rainwater. With the blotter-like plant cover gone,

THE WORK OF CONSERVATIONISTS

Conservationists work to preserve nature for future generations. People concerned with conservation seek not only to maintain a high-quality environment suitable for both wildlife and humans, but also to preserve the natural biological, genetic, and habitat diversity of ecosystems. This often involves preventing or minimizing environmental pollution from industrial, agricultural, urban, and domestic sources, including toxic chemicals, radioactive waste, and elevated water temperatures. Conservationists also seek to prevent the waste of natural resources of any sort, reduce consumption of energy and unnecessary commercial products, and support recycling efforts.

many rivers flooded at unprecedented levels when the winter snows melted. During natural drought periods, wells ran dry and crops died in the fields. Dust storms blew the topsoil away. Birds, fish, and other wildlife that once had thrived in the forests, fields, and streams became scarce. Some kinds became extinct, vanishing forever. These negative experiences gradually led the growing nation to recognize some of its environmental problems, ultimately leading to some of the world's strongest and most effective conservation programs.

Making Better Use of Natural Resources

Worldwide, the abuses of the past—many of which continue into the present—have shown the need for a more sensible use of natural resources. For instance, there is the case of the logging company that cuts down too many trees without replanting for the future or regard for the welfare of all native wildlife that are affected; the industrial plant that fouls a river or pollutes the air with its waste; the large commercial farms that use pesticides and herbicides without concern for their environmental impact,

Toxic plumes billow from smokestacks in St. Petersburg, Russia. Industrial plants are a major source of air pollution. AFP/Getty Images

injuring not only their own natural communities but also those downstream. All are abusing natural resources.

Conservation groups have promoted legislation that corrects these abuses, and instituted legal proceedings against violators. People have been made increasingly aware that their continued existence depends on these and other efforts to stop environmental

RECYCLING

The recovery and reuse of materials from spent products—called recycling or materials salvage—is an ancient practice with many modern applications. In recent years recycling has become a major part of environmental policy, largely owing to increased costs of solid- and hazardous-waste disposal, the scarcity of natural resources, and growing concern over polluted land, water, and air.

There are two types of recycling operations: internal and external. In internal recycling, an industry reclaims materials that are a waste product of a manufacturing process and reuses them within the same process. Internal recycling is common in the metals industry, for example. External recycling is the reclaiming of materials from a product that has been worn out or rendered obsolete. An example of external recycling is the collection of old newspapers and magazines for the manufacture of newsprint or other paper products.

deterioration. Educating the public on the need to make better use of natural resources is vitally important, since public attitudes can have a measurable direct effect on conservation efforts. In the early 21st century, for example, surveys in the United States revealed that more than 60 percent of citizens purchase recyclable products when given a choice. Such information will ultimately lead to companies supporting recycling because it has become more economically profitable to do so.

CHAPTER 2
WATER AND FOREST CONSERVATION

Water is an essential natural resource and is a frequent focus of conservation efforts. Everyone uses it. Water is needed in homes for drinking, cooking, washing clothes and dishes, and bathing. It also is used for non-vital activities such as filling home swimming pools, watering lawns, and washing vehicles. Communities must have water for fire protection. People also use it for recreational activities such as swimming, boating, and fishing. Industries use water to produce electricity, cool machinery, and perform a large number of manufacturing processes. Some agricultural systems use vast quantities of water for crops during the growing season.

Also among the most valuable of nature's resources are forests. A shelter for many forms of wildlife, they also play a key role in the maintenance of watersheds that are essential to water and soil conservation. They supply lumber for construction, cordwood for fuel, and pulp for paper. Forests also provide the

An irrigation system waters farmland. Large farms are major consumers of water. Shutterstock.com

raw materials used in many synthetic products considered essential for modern life, including fibers, plastics, and medicines.

WATER CONSERVATION: PAST, PRESENT, AND FUTURE

Water has been recognized since Babylonian times as one of the most valuable and vital resources for all living things, including humans. Ancient Mesopotamian laws about

In the 1960s, the United States Postal Service issued a stamp that showed the cycle of water usage and promoted water conservation. **Shutterstock.com**

water use during drought periods designated who got to use water and how they could use it. Such laws were a form of conservation in that they were designed to assure the preservation of a limited environmental resource. Conflicts over water started long ago, and predictions are that they are going to get even worse in the near future as human populations increase in many parts of the world.

To minimize such conflicts, water conservation measures are likely to become commonplace in many regions, even in some places where water is now taken for granted. A dilemma for conservationists is how to deal with the wants and needs of humans for water during long periods of drought. Critical levels of water are required in lakes, streams, and rivers of a region for the basic needs of populated areas. But choices involving water diversion from one region to another involve balancing not only the competing needs of different communities, but also options of using the water for power production, recreational activities, and the survival of some species of fish and other wildlife.

Watersheds and Their Importance

A watershed is the area drained by a river or a stream in a region. Such an area slopes toward a common land trough. Some rain runs off, or drains, over the ground surface. Runoff water forms small streams, which flow into larger ones. These eventually join to form a river, which may lead to a lake, reservoir, or ocean.

A natural watershed conserves water. It has clear streams and an ample cover of trees, grasses, and other plants. Plants help contribute to form a part of the topsoil called humus, which consists of decaying leaves and wood, bacteria, dead insects, and other plant and animal remains. Humus provides some of the nutrients for new plant life and many soil invertebrates. Together with a network of roots, it acts as a blotter that soaks up rain. Plants break the force of falling rain and

River water running down a forested slope. Nature has the ability to conserve water via areas with clean running water and plenty of surrounding vegetation. **Shutterstock.com**

scatter the drops over leaves and branches. Some of the water returns to the air by evaporation. Part of the water used by plants is passed through their leaves into the air again by transpiration.

Any remaining water that does not flow to streams sinks into the earth through countless tiny channels. Some of the spaces in the soil through which water percolates are caused by natural features of the geology or soil itself. Others are made by plant roots and burrowing animals such as earthworms, insects, and moles.

The level at which the earth is permanently saturated is known as the water table. This vast underground water supply fluctuates with the seasons and the amount of rainfall. During long, heavy rains the soil may not be able to soak up all the water. Some of it runs off the surface, but in a forested watershed it moves slowly. Deep snow that melts slowly allows water to soak into the soil gradually.

The Consequences of Mismanaged Watersheds

When all the trees in an area have been cut down (clear-cut) owing to poor forestry practices, or when grasses and other plants have been stripped off by fire, overgrazing, or poor farming practices, the watershed suffers. The water from rainfall flows over the ground's surface instead of being absorbed by the vegetation and organic materials that would be present on a natural forest floor.

When there are no leaves, branches, or grasses to break the force of falling rain and the blotter of roots and humus is gone, mud closes the channels through which water

A silt-filled river in Australia, showing the effects of pollution and soil runoff. Eco Images/Universal Images Group/Getty Images

sinks into the soil. If the land is level, the water stands in stagnant pools; if it slopes, the water runs downhill into the rivers. Streams in a mismanaged watershed become brown with silt, or suspended soil, because the racing water carries soil along with it.

A mismanaged, unvegetated watershed can result in destructive floods in the spring because heavy rains and melting snows reach rivers too quickly and overflow the banks downstream. In the summer, streams, springs, and wells can dry up because little or no water has sunk into the underground reservoirs.

Water Pollution

The silting of streams is a form of water pollution. Heavy siltation in streams and rivers kills fish and other aquatic animals, including tadpoles, mollusks, and larval insects, indirectly by reducing the amount of oxygen in the water. As the flowing water slows, silt is deposited on streambeds, and the natural flow patterns of waterways become altered. Reservoirs behind dams eventually fill with silt unless erosion is stopped in watersheds above.

Other kinds of water pollution have created other problems. Many waterways are used as dumps for household and industrial wastes. Some communities dump untreated sewage and garbage into the nearest streams. Industries contaminate the waterways when they discharge acids, chemicals, greases, oils, and organic matter into them. Such materials foul drinking water and endanger public health. They destroy commercial fisheries. They also make waterways unusable for recreational purposes. Leaks and spills from offshore oil wells and wrecked or damaged oil

Bags of garbage litter a stream in Kiev, Ukraine. Trash dumping is one of the most common forms of water pollution. **Shutterstock.com**

tankers have caused the widespread destruction of marine life.

The large-scale use of organic insecticides, herbicides, toxic metals, and pesticides has polluted streams and destroyed wildlife. Some pesticides tend to concentrate in the tissues of plants and animals in nature's food chains. Thus organisms at the ends of these chains, including humans, may take in harmful amounts of pesticides deposited in their food supply.

Forest Threats and Conservation

Fire can be a major scourge of a forest, especially if natural fires have been suppressed in a region. Although lightning is sometimes responsible for kindling forest fires, human carelessness is most often the cause. Ground fires can destroy the organic soil of the forest and render it incapable of supporting tree life. Also, elimination of the understory leaves bare soil, making it more susceptible to water and wind erosion. When crown fires rage through the leafy tops of trees, they destroy timber and its resident wildlife. However, fire is a natural occurrence in many regions, and most forests rebound from occasional fires and the wildlife returns.

A common tool of foresters is the use of prescribed burning (sometimes known as controlled burning) to attempt to imitate the natural burning cycle of forests in a region. The purpose is to burn off leaf or pine needle litter and fallen twigs on the ground's surface to return nutrients to the soil. Occasional burning also prevents the buildup of such organic fuels, which can result in major forest fires that cannot be controlled. Prescribed burning presents a dilemma for forest managers and timber companies in some areas. Prescribed burns in populated areas near forests can send smoke into nearby homes, resulting in complaints from homeowners. However, foresters receive worse criticism when a forest fire becomes a completely unmanageable crown fire that burns down houses because prescribed burning was not done and natural burning cycles were suppressed.

Insect infestation can also threaten the life of a forest. In the United States, the Forest Pest Control Act of 1947 authorized surveys of public and private forests so that insect-borne diseases of trees could be detected and suppressed before they became epidemic.

A more serious threat than fire or insects is indiscriminate logging. When every tree

of a stand is cut without any provision for natural reseeding or manual replanting, as is still common in many parts of the world, particularly the tropics, no canopy is left to protect the soil against the splash erosion of rainfall. The loose soil soon becomes deposited as silt in nearby streams. Timber must be treated as a renewable crop, carefully harvested to ensure a sustained yield of trees. In this way, a balance is struck between the cutting of mature trees and the growth of saplings. A major problem with forest removal in tropical areas is that no topsoil layer is present to promote natural reseeding. In the tropics, most of the nutrients are aboveground in the vegetation itself, rather than stored in the soil as is typical of temperate-zone forests. Thus, different forestry techniques must be used to assure conservation of tropical forests.

A fire manager starts a prescribed burn in Yellowstone National Park, in the northwestern United States. Such fires are intentionally set to mimic the natural burn cycles of forests and to prevent the buildup of dead plant matter on the ground, which can fuel dangerous crown fires. **Bryan Harry/NPS**

CHAPTER 3
Soil Conservation

Whenever land is stripped of its plant cover, soil is inevitably lost by erosion, the so-called silent thief. A single rainstorm can wash away centuries-old accumulations of soil from neglected or badly managed fields. Topsoil is an extremely valuable natural resource. Under this thin blanket of rich dirt and humus, in which plants grow best, is a less fertile material called subsoil. If the surface layer of topsoil is blown or washed away, the remaining subsoil cannot support plant life. The submarginal farms must eventually be abandoned.

Types of Soil Erosion

In the late 1900s more than 700 million acres (283 million hectares) of agricultural land in the United States were subject to erosion. Some 230 million acres (93 million hectares) of cropland required constant supervision to control erosion caused by wind and water.

An abandoned farmstead in the Dust Bowl of Oklahoma in 1937 shows the effects of wind erosion. **USDA Photo**

Dust storms are the evidence of wind erosion. Soil unprotected by plant cover simply blows away. During the 1930s millions of acres of U.S. farmlands were badly damaged by wind. Many fields lost from 2 to 12 inches (5 to 30 centimeters) of vital topsoil during this period. As a result, the entire southern Great Plains area was called the Dust Bowl.

One of the several kinds of water erosion is sheet erosion—the wasting away of level land in thin layers. The deterioration may go on for years without being noticed, though the land yields successively smaller crops. A patch of subsoil showing through on some

Llamas and alpacas graze in the foothills of the Payachata mountains in Bolivia. When livestock eat too much of an area's vegetation, the risk of topsoil erosion increases. Aizar Raldes/AFP/Getty Images

slight rise of ground may be the first sign that the land is nearly finished as a food producer.

Splash erosion is the washing away of soil by the direct battering of rain. In rill erosion, runoff digs small channels called rills in the soil. The little rills run together, form a network of larger rills, and then develop into gullies. When gully erosion occurs, the land can become as unproductive as a desert.

Conservationists also recognize that livestock can overgraze a plot of land until severe soil erosion occurs. In the late 1900s about 4 million acres (1.6 million hectares) of topsoil were lost every year through erosion, and about 85 percent was estimated to be the result of overgrazing by livestock.

Although major losses of productive agricultural lands occurred in the first half of the 20th century because of erosion, a major concern in the 21st century is the loss of natural soils and habitats as a result of commercial development. Large tracts of productive land—estimated as high as 1 million acres (400,000 hectares) each year—continue to be lost through the building of roads, suburban housing, and industrial and other commercial site developments, including airport expansion.

EROSION ON URBAN LAND

Cropland is not the only land with soil subject to erosion. The land on which housing and other urban projects are built is particularly susceptible because its protective cover is generally removed.

To prevent erosion on construction sites, builders should take corrective action. For example, mulches placed on steeply excavated slopes usually prevent soil from washing or blowing away. Straw or fiber netting may be used as mulches. On sites where erosion control is more difficult, hydroseeding can be used. Grass seed, fertilizer, and mulch are power-sprayed on excavated slopes. The quick-growing grass then stabilizes the soil against erosion. Many bridge and highway construction projects use silt fences below the disturbed areas to trap loose soil and prevent runoff into nearby streams.

SOIL CONSERVATION IN AGRICULTURE

Government agencies in many countries have developed soil and land classification systems. In the United States the Soil Erosion Service (soon renamed the Soil Conservation Service) was created in 1933 as a major division of the United States Department of Agriculture. The Soil Conservation Service (now called the Natural Resources Conservation Service [NRCS]) devised a land classification system that offered guidance in the proper use of land. Such factors as slope, type of soil, amount of rainfall, humidity, and vegetation type were considered when determining land use for maximum productivity.

Of the eight land classifications, classes I, II, III, and IV were considered appropriate for cultivated crops, although classes III and IV required skillful management to avoid serious erosion. Classes V through VII could be used for forests and for grazing. Class VIII land, which included sandy shores and extremely rocky places, was considered suitable only for wildlife or scenic and recreational purposes. The NRCS uses a modification of the same system today.

Covering the ground with plants is one of the key elements in soil conservation. To test this, the Department of Agriculture experimented with two steep plots of adjacent land, one planted with crops and the other thickly covered with grass. The cultivated plot lost 7 inches (18 centimeters) of topsoil in 11 years. By contrast, it was estimated that it would

A sapling tree grows in Senegal, planted by rangers in an attempt to keep the land fertile and conserve soil. Seyllou/AFP/Getty Images

take 34,000 years to lose the same amount of topsoil from the grass-covered plot.

Plant cover tends to reduce raindrop energy and hold rainwater where it falls, thus preventing the soil from blowing or washing away. Gullies can be healed in many cases by planting new plants. They provide a tangle of leaves and stems that trap and hold in place part of the soil carried by runoff. Another way to heal gullies is to build brush dams across them at regular intervals. Then soil and water running down the gully are caught behind the dams and held in place.

To help prevent the start of erosion, farmers have used a variety of conservation measures. The effectiveness of each depends on the climate, topography, and soil type.

METHODS OF SOIL PREPARATION

Contouring involves plowing, planting, and cultivating sloping fields around hillsides, with curving furrows horizontal to the hill, instead of furrows running straight uphill and downhill. The curved furrows catch rainfall and allow much of it to soak into the ground. They also catch soil washing down from higher levels. On long slopes a low ridge, or terrace, thrown along the outer side of the slope catches soil and rainwater and retards runoff. Encouraging plant growth on a terrace will help hold soil.

In dry regions a lister plow can be used to throw a ridge of dirt to each side, creating a trough about 18 inches (46 centimeters) wide and 7 inches (18 centimeters) deep. Crops are planted in the bottom of the trough.

Trees line a wheat field. Planting trees near farmland creates a shield that protects crops and topsoil from the effects of the wind. Shutterstock.com

Another soil conservation measure involves the use of windrows. On treeless plains, rows of trees are planted at the edges of fields to break the force of winds across the fields and reduce wind erosion.

Deep tillage, or stubble mulching, may also be used. Instead of turning over the soil with a moldboard or no-till plow, a deep-tillage plow breaks the soil below the surface. It leaves the surface vegetation or harvest remains from the previous crop to act as a cover.

Use of Crops in Conservation

In the method of soil conservation known as strip cropping, strips of close-growing plants, such as grasses or clover, are alternated between strips of clean-tilled row crops, such as corn and soybeans. The strips of close-growing plants hold water and keep it from eroding the cultivated strip below. These strips are planted on the contour.

Crop rotation, which involves planting different crops each year on a piece of land, keeps the soil productive. One crop can benefit the next. For example, nitrogen is essential for plant growth and is added to the soil by nitrogen-producing legumes, such as clover, alfalfa, soybeans, and cowpeas. These combine nitrogen from the air with other elements and store it in the soil through their roots. In a year or two the plants can be plowed under. This is called green manuring.

After the roots have rotted, other plants that need nitrogen but cannot use nitrogen

Strips of grass alternate with rows of crops in the soil conservation process known as contour strip farming. Shutterstock.com

in the air—for example, corn and potatoes—can use the nitrogen stored in the soil for growth. Rotations are programmed with strip-cropping by shifting the close-growing strips and the tilled strips at fixed intervals.

The use of cover crops can also be beneficial. In this practice, land is kept covered in winter and summer with either a growing crop or the residue, such as corn stalks, from the crop previously grown. When cover crops are plowed under for green manuring, the plant foods added to the soil improve its water-holding capacity and increase its fertility.

CHAPTER 4
Wildlife Conservation

The preservation of wildlife greatly depends upon water and soil conservation. The native plants and animals constitute the wildlife of a region and are a product of the land resources and habitat conditions. But, like humans, wild animals must have food, water, and shelter. Destroying the forests, marshes, ponds, and grasslands alters their food and water supplies and the places in which they live, hibernate, and reproduce.

Impact of Human Activity

Wildlife conservationists generally recognize five distinct but interacting categories of environmental impact that need to be considered in regard to how human activities affect native wildlife in the broadest sense (all wild animals and plants). They are habitat loss and degradation, introduced species, pollution, disease and parasitism, and unsustainable use.

Habitat Loss and Degradation

The loss and degradation of natural habitat is the single most important factor contributing to declines and destruction of populations and species in most regions of the world. Although examples of other specific causes can be given, the destruction of terrestrial and aquatic habitat through agricultural, urban, and industrial development is generally agreed to be the main cause of declines in native wildlife species. Highway construction and traffic have caused immeasurable loss of natural habitat and direct wildlife mortality, especially in the United States. For example, the total surface area of paved U.S. highways is more than the area of the state of Indiana.

Introduction of Exotic and Invasive Species

Scientists have documented that introductions of nonnative species of plants and animals have resulted in the declines and elimination of native species in some regions. An example in the early 2000s is the destruction of North American hemlock trees by the Asian woolly adelgid

A wildlife specialist holds a brown tree snake that was captured on a military base in Guam as part of a program to prevent the species from spreading to Hawaii. Master Sgt. Lance Cheung/U.S. Air Force

insect. Tropical exotic lizards introduced into southern Florida have established populations that outcompete or prey on native species. Numbers of native lizards have declined noticeably, especially in areas where natural habitat has been replaced by houses and other man-made structures.

The United States Geological Survey has a Web page describing the problems caused by the brown tree snake. After the species was accidentally introduced to Guam in the mid-20th century, it colonized the island and preyed relentlessly on native species, causing the decline, local elimination, or extinction of several species of birds, fruit bats, and lizards.

Environmental Pollution

Numerous toxic chemicals and metals that are by-products of industry and agriculture have direct and indirect negative effects on wildlife. Agricultural areas release contaminants such as fertilizers, pesticides, and herbicides into waterways upon which fish and terrestrial wildlife depend. Other environmental contaminants detrimental to aquatic wildlife include runoff of petroleum products from highways and domestic effluents from urban and suburban areas.

For example, many coastal salt marshes and estuaries of the Atlantic Ocean and Gulf of Mexico have become dumping grounds for litter and industrial effluents. Too many coastal areas have been used for commercial

Runoff soil and water from farm irrigation is dumped into the Florida Everglades. The pesticides and fertilizer in this muddy mix are harmful to fish and other aquatic wildlife. Cameron Davidson/Workbook Stock/Getty Images

developments including resort housing, golf courses, and boat marinas. Continued exploitation of the coastal salt marshes will further reduce the number of wildlife species, including diamondback terrapins, salt marsh snakes, and marsh wrens.

Disease and Parasitism

A wide variety of parasites and diseases are known or suspected to be responsible for illnesses that weaken many plant and animal wildlife species. Wildlife conservation biologists have concluded that the levels of resistance of many species are lower than normal because the species are already stressed from other environmental impacts such as natural habitat destruction or chemical pollution.

Unsustainable Use

All human cultures have used wild plants and animals as a part of their existence, not only for the necessities of food, clothing, and shelter but also for recreation and leisure activities. However, actions such as timbering at unsustainable levels and overharvesting for food and the commercial pet trade has plagued numerous species of plants and animals on a global scale. The dramatic loss of millions of acres of tropical rainforest in the Americas, Africa, and Asia has driven hundreds of species to extinction. In the early 21st century the unregulated commercial trade in edible Asian freshwater turtles, sold as a delicacy, was documented by conservation biologists to exceed any

Turtles put on sale as meat in a Chinese market. Scientists predict that freshwater turtles will soon become extinct if such practices continue at current levels. **Andrew Wong/Getty Images**

possible sustainable levels. Many of the species were already recognized as endangered, and their extinction in the wild is expected early in the century unless such activities are curtailed.

An additional category of concern for wildlife conservationists, despite political debates about the issue, is global climatic change. Many climatologists predict major changes in temperature and rainfall patterns in many regions. Such changes will result in habitat modifications that could affect most wildlife in minor or major ways, and will become the focus of many wildlife conservation efforts.

Another area that needs to be considered is the disappearance of populations or reduction in numbers of species not directly related to any of the causes mentioned, but that may be natural in occurrence. Of course, such an unexplained decline of a species may have been made worse in an indirect or undetectable manner by human activities, or may be a cumulative effect of several unidentified causes. The role of wildlife conservation is to identify and minimize the impact of human-caused activities that are controllable through a combination of regulation, management, and education.

Endangered Species

Plants and animals have become extinct and new species have evolved since life on Earth began. Early human cultures may have caused the extinction of some species, but the primary causes for species to become extinct were natural ones. Major environmental changes resulted in the eventual disappearance of species unable to adapt to new conditions. Well-known natural extinctions include that of the dinosaurs and many other species represented in the fossil record.

Natural forces are still at work, but human activities cause most of the rapid and widespread environmental changes that affect plants and animals today. Many species have been unable to make the biological adjustments necessary for survival. Thus more species than ever before are threatened with extinction.

Endangered in the United States

Of the original native wildlife of the United States, many species are now extinct. These include the passenger pigeon, the Carolina parakeet, the great auk, the Labrador

Because the species is now extinct, people can only see the great auk in old photographs such as this, taken at the beginning of the 20th century. Hulton Archive/Getty Images

duck, the Pallas cormorant, the dusky seaside sparrow, and the heath hen. Mammals gone forever include the Eastern elk, the Plains wolf, the sea mink, and the Badlands bighorn.

Many smaller birds and mammals have also become extinct in the wild. Several species of mountaintop salamanders with small geographic ranges in the Appalachian Mountains are assumed to have been wiped out during strip mining activities of the past. The number of certain United States reptiles, including bog turtles, indigo snakes, southern hognose snakes, and northern cricket frogs, grows smaller every year. Many game species are now protected by law from overhunting and overfishing.

Endangered Species Worldwide

Worldwide, the World Conservation Union (also called the IUCN) keeps track of species threatened with extinction. Endangered species include many of the world's great cats, whales, rhinoceroses, tapirs, and many other mammals, birds, and reptiles. However, housing and other facilities needed by an expanding human population are encroaching on their habitats.

Customs officials in Thailand display African elephant tusks that were brought into the country illegally. Poachers have killed thousands of African elephants for the ivory, endangering the existence of the species. **Pornchai Kittiwongsakul/AFP/Getty Images**

In addition, many species are the victims of the illegal pet trade and of the trade in exotic pelts and skins. The African elephant, once common throughout the sub-Saharan region of the African continent, has been greatly reduced in numbers because of illegal poaching for the ivory trade.

An alligator basks in the sun on a sandy beach. In the United States, alligators are a wildlife conservation success story. **Shutterstock.com**

PROTECTING WILDLIFE IN THE UNITED STATES

The United States Fish and Wildlife Service maintains a list of endangered and threatened species of the United States. Environmental concerns for a variety of nongame reptiles, amphibians, small fishes, insects, and mollusks, as well as other animals and plants, is reflected in the number of species classed as threatened or endangered. Some states also have laws and regulations that protect many of these species. However, many continue to be threatened by habitat destruction.

In the United States the Endangered Species Act has been effective for preserving some species that seemed destined for extinction. For example, the American alligator had been reduced to a relatively small number by the early 1960s because of overhunting for hides and meat. After 20 years of protection, the species recovered to a large extent. By the early 2000s, coastal states where alligators are abundant allowed limited hunting of the species.

Wildlife Conservation Organizations

Many nonprofit conservation organizations have been formed to protect nongame species. Some focus on single species, and others on natural groupings of organisms. Two successful programs established in the 1990s are Partners in Flight (PIF) and Partners in Amphibian and Reptile Conservation (PARC). PIF emphasizes conservation of land birds, while PARC is the largest program addressing

WHY PRESERVE?

The 1973 Endangered Species Act addressed the issue of why an endangered species of plant or animal should be offered formal protection. As stated in the act, such species "are of esthetic, ecological, educational, historical, recreational, and scientific value to the Nation and its people." Numerous species are medically or agriculturally significant because of their unique properties or traits. It cannot be predicted when a species might be discovered to be of direct value to humans. Once a species becomes extinct, any benefits it might have provided are lost forever.

As scientists unravel the intricate network of plant-animal relationships in the natural world, more and more species are discovered to have a vital, and often unsuspected, dependence on other species. Obviously, if the extinction of one species is permitted through rapid, human-caused activities that do not permit natural adaptations and evolution to occur, certain other species may also be affected. This can result in a "domino effect" of potential extinctions.

Through breeding programs and reintroduction of animals into their natural habitats, several species have been brought back from the brink of extinction, including the black-footed ferret and the California condor, though both are still endangered. Several more species are undergoing such programs, and they will eventually be reintroduced into the wild.

conservation of both amphibians and reptiles. Both organizations have a U.S. focus but are international in scope. Other major conservation organizations that protect wildlife and their ecosystems worldwide include Conservation International, the Wildlife Conservation Society, and the International Crane Foundation, and, in the United States, Defenders of Wildlife and the National Wildlife Federation.

Further aid for vanishing species comes from private organizations involved in educating the public about environmental issues. Many organizations promote species preservation through magazines, lecture series, Web sites, and television programs. In addition, many groups lobby legislators to support protection laws. Some also take more direct action. The Nature Conservancy, for example, buys and preserves tracts of habitat vital to endangered species. WWF (formerly the World Wildlife Fund) monitors the illegal trade in endangered animals and helps establish reserves for threatened wildlife, among many other projects. The primary tactic of Greenpeace has been "direct, nonviolent actions," such as steering small inflatable craft between the harpoon guns of whalers and their endangered prey.

Migratory birds gather on the water at the Merritt Island National Wildlife Refuge in Titusville, Florida. Stan Honda/AFP/Getty Images

REFUGES FOR WILDLIFE

Some governments have established national wildlife reservations and game refuges. Many refuges are established in places to which animals, especially migratory birds, have long been attracted. In the United States, many of these are administered by the Fish and Wildlife Service.

All U.S. national parks and national monuments, operated by the National Park Service, serve as wildlife refuges.

Individuals can help restore wildlife to the countryside simply by providing birds, fish, and other animals with natural feeding, breeding, and refuge sites. They can do even more by encouraging their state and federal governments to provide effective laws for habitat protection.

Brush piles scattered through a woodlot provide retreats for cottontails, weasels, mink, and woodchucks. Whether natural or man-made, small wetlands without fish provide breeding habitat for frogs and salamanders and feeding areas for turtles, snakes, and aquatic insects. Fencerows (undeveloped land on either side of a fence) can provide a haven for many kinds of birds.

CHAPTER 5
Mineral and Fossil Fuel Conservation

Minerals and fossil fuels are nonrenewable resources. Once exhausted, they can never be replaced. The United States has valuable stores of coal, oil, natural gas, and minerals. Until the U.S. Mineral Leasing Act was passed in 1920, the resources on public lands were transferred to private individuals, who sometimes exploited them, meaning used them carelessly. Today, in many countries worldwide, including the United States, government regulation attempts to assure that private industry makes proper use of these resources. In some countries, the government itself operates key mining industries.

Limited Supply

For years coal was mined as though it were inexhaustible—about one ton wasted for each ton mined. Various government agencies have promoted more efficient mining

Inside a coal mine. Because of their limited supply, fossil fuels, such as coal, are a prime target of conservation efforts. **Shutterstock.com**

methods. In addition, the use of other sources of energy in home construction and in industry, and to generate electricity, has greatly extended the life of the coal supply. Natural gas and petroleum were once carelessly wasted also. In earlier days, for example, because no use for natural gas had been found, it was burned off or allowed to escape into the air.

Like other conservation needs, the wise management of mineral resources has become more pressing because of the growing number of consumers. As the human population increases, the demand increases for more consumer goods, such as household appliances and automobiles. Manufacturers meet these rising demands from already dwindling deposits of metal ore and fuels.

The U.S. Energy Crisis

Throughout most of its history the United States has had ample, inexpensive supplies of fuels to provide energy. During the 20th century the country gradually shifted from reliance on coal as its principal fuel to dependence on natural gas and petroleum. By the late 1970s the United States was consuming more than one third of the world's supply of these two fuels and was dependent on them for three fourths of its energy.

As it became more apparent during the 1970s that natural gas and petroleum resources might be depleted within the foreseeable future, energy conservation became an important government policy. Conservation measures were also adopted

***The AMC Gremlin, a small car that used less gas, was developed partly in response to energy conservation measures put forth by the U.S. government in the 1970s.* Hulton Archive/Getty Images**

because of political and economic developments. About one half of the petroleum used by the United States was imported, much of it from Middle Eastern countries that opposed certain United States foreign policies. In addition, oil-exporting countries increased oil prices by more than 1,500 percent between 1970 and 1980.

In response, government, industry, and private citizens all took steps to conserve energy. To meet new government standards, smaller and more efficient automobiles were produced. There was renewed emphasis on improving the country's mass transportation systems. Grants, loans, and tax credits were offered for the installation of insulation and other energy-saving devices in homes and commercial properties. Efficiency standards for appliances were adopted. The government mandated minimum and maximum temperatures for nonresidential buildings and suggested maintenance of similar temperatures in homes.

U.S. Energy Legislation of the '70s

In 1977 President Jimmy Carter established a Cabinet-level Department of Energy (which took over some of the functions of the Atomic Energy Commission) and proposed a comprehensive energy program. As passed by Congress in 1978, the program included measures to discourage energy consumption, particularly of natural gas and petroleum, and provided incentives for alternative energy sources. An Energy Security Act, to develop synthetic fuels, was passed in 1980.

Conservation Efforts

Some mineral resources, particularly metals, may be recycled so that they can be salvaged and reused. The recycling of waste metals is an important conservation practice that has become a major business. It is known as secondary production. Conservation programs for fossil fuels include reducing their use, such as by replacing them with more abundant and cleaner sources of energy.

Circuit boards from discarded computers are recycled for secondary materials. Copper, iron, aluminum, nickel, tin, and lead can all be extracted from used computers and other electronics. Dibyangshu Sarkar/AFP/Getty Images

Signs mark fields in Illinois where corn is grown to make ethanol, a type of alternative fuel. Scott Olson/Getty Images

Alternative Fuels

The energy crisis of the 1970s led to increased emphasis on alternative sources of power. The government supported further development of solar, geothermal, and wind power. Industries and utilities were encouraged, and in certain circumstances required, to use coal as an alternative to natural gas and petroleum. The government encouraged

Renault debuts its electric car in Tel Aviv, Israel. Several car companies are experimenting with models that run on electricity, in combination with or instead of gasoline, to conserve fossil fuels. Getty Images

long-range research programs, including the development of economical methods of producing gas and oil from coal and shale. Gasohol—a mixture of ethanol (alcohol produced from grain or other plant matter) and gasoline—was tried as an alternative fuel for automobiles, and electric cars were developed.

With the election of Ronald Reagan as president in 1980, government support for most of those programs was ended. Instead, the government promoted the expansion of nuclear energy and a return to imported petroleum. In the early 2000s the United States used fossil fuels to meet roughly 85 percent of its energy needs, with nuclear power accounting for about another 8 percent.

Worldwide, growing concern about global warming in the early 21st century led to greater efforts to reduce the use of fossil fuels and to rely increasingly on renewable, nonpolluting energy sources such as solar, wind, and geothermal power. New methods of using biomass energy, by burning plant matter or producing ethanol and other fuels from crops and agricultural wastes, were also investigated, and more electric and gasoline-electric hybrid automobiles were introduced.

Conservation and the Environment

Conservation programs call for lessening instances of environmental pollution, habitat degradation, and erosion caused by mining, processing, and using mineral products. Mining wastes are often rich in sulfuric acid, for example, and their runoff into streams can devastate communities of plants and animals living in the water and nearby. Without proper land reclamation programs, which restore areas as close to their original condition as possible, surface mining for coal and other minerals can strip off the fertile topsoil in an area and leave behind an abandoned wasteland in which few, if any, plants can grow.

Conservationists survey the water quality in a mine water filtration pond, which is designed to remove toxins from mining wastewater. **Bob Nichols/USDA Natural Resources Conservation Service**

Coal burning can create pollution problems, not only in the atmosphere but also for organisms, especially amphibians and fish, living in aquatic systems. In addition, the burning of coal, oil, and natural gas, such as in power plants, factories, and motor vehicles, also releases the greenhouse gas carbon dioxide into the air; most scientists believe that this is the major cause of global warming.

Conclusion

Conservation is everyone's responsibility. Each member of a community can take steps toward conserving or safeguarding the natural resources in their area. Simple ways of doing so include recycling, reducing waste by choosing reusable products instead of disposable ones, limiting water use in the home and yard, planting trees and shrubs, putting up a birdhouse or bird feeder, and driving less by walking, biking, or using mass transit whenever possible. Additionally, if conservation efforts are lax or lacking in one's community, one may encourage local, state, or federal officials to establish effective programs to manage and preserve natural resources.

A few individuals or companies can cause major setbacks in conservation programs, however. In many instances stringent laws and regulations must be passed and effectively enforced to stop the degradation and destruction of natural resources that bring gain to particular individuals or corporations but no environmental benefits to society.

Surveys in the early part of the 21st century have revealed that Americans are more concerned about the environment than ever before. Society appears to be collectively expressing the view that conservation of natural resources is an important topic for discussion, and a cause worthy of our time and effort.

aquatic Having to do with bodies of water.

conservation Taking care of the environment in a way that preserves natural ecosystems while taking into account human needs for production and recreation.

cultivate To prepare for or see through a period of growth.

degradation Experiencing a decline to a very lowly state.

erosion When Earth's topsoil is blown away by wind or washed away by water.

estuary A waterway where two or more rivers or streams meet, acting as a passageway to the ocean.

evaporation The process of a liquid converting to a vapor.

extinct No longer existing.

habitat A place where plants and animals, or a community of organisms, live, including all living and nonliving factors or conditions of the surrounding environment.

hybrid Something that is created using elements from different sources to make a whole; a composite.

invasive species An organism that is introduced to an area it does not normally belong in, which usually causes problems and harm to native creatures and plants.

parasite An animal or plant that lives off another organism in a one-sided way in a relationship that is beneficial only to the parasite.

prescribed burning Fires that are purposely set to burn off organic litter on the forest floor in order to return nutrients to the soil.

silt Bits of rock and clay that can pollute streams and rivers.

stewardship To be responsible for taking care of or managing something.

sustainability A method of harvesting or using a resource so that the resource is not depleted or permanently damaged.

terrestrial Of or relating to land and earth.

transpiration The act of passing vapor from a living body.

watershed An area from which all precipitation flows to a single stream or set of streams.

windrow A long mound of organic refuse that is turned into compost when tended.

For More Information

Canadian Wildlife Federation
350 Michael Cowpland Drive
Kanata, ON K2M 2W1
Canada
(800) 563-9453
Web site: http://www.cwf-fcf.org/en
Protecting Canadian wildlife and its native habitats is the mission of the Canadian Wildlife Federation. Awareness programs, general information, and how-to tips are the tools of the organization's trade.

Conservation International
2011 Crystal Drive, Suite 500
Arlington, VA 22202
(800) 429-5660
Web site: http://www.conservation.org
The organization's name says it all. Conservation International aims to protect resources and address issues of climate, fresh water, and biodiversity issues that affect communities around the world.

David Suzuki Society
219 – 2211 West 4th Avenue
Vancouver, BC V6K 4S2
Canada
(800) 453-1533

Web site: http://www.davidsuzuki.org
Diversity and sustainability are the watchwords of the David Suzuki Society. Based in Canada, the organization provides science-based education and advocacy toward preserving the country's natural resources.

Earthwatch Institute
114 Western Avenue
Boston, MA 02134
(800) 776-0188
Web site: http://www.earthwatch.org
Earthwatch Institute offers a three-step approach to conservation: Plan a strategy, conduct research, and get people involved. In addition to research and general information, the organization arranges scientific expeditions that amateur conservationists can join and get firsthand experience.

Nature Canada
75 Albert Street, Suite 300
Ottawa, ON K1P 5E7
Canada
(800) 267-4088
Web site: http://www.naturecanada.ca

The nonprofit agency Nature Canada seeks to protect wildlife and natural habitats throughout Canada. Outreach programs, publications, and volunteer support are the primary means the organization uses to reach its goals.

Nature Conservancy
4245 North Fairfax Drive, Suite 100
Arlington, VA 22203-1606
(703) 841-5400
Web site: http://www.nature.org
A leading conservation organization based in the United States, The Nature Conservancy seeks to protect and preserve animals, plants, and natural habitats around the globe.

WWF (formerly World Wildlife Fund)
U.S. Headquarters
1250 Twenty-Fourth Street NW
P.O. Box 97180
Washington, DC 20090-7180
(202) 293-4800
Web site: http://www.worldwildlife.org
Saving the natural world for future generations is the aim of WWF. The organization is noted for scientific

research and advocacy initiatives on a host of conservation-related topics, with a special emphasis on wildlife and natural habitats.

Web Sites

Due to the changing nature of Internet links, Rosen Educational Services has developed an online list of Web sites related to the subject of this book. This site is updated regularly. Please use this link to access the list:

http://www.rosenlinks.com/teos/prot

Calhoun, Yael, ed. *Conservation* (Chelsea House, 2005).

Cruden, Gabriel. *Energy Alternatives* (Lucent, 2005).

Dalgleish, Sharon. *Managing the Land*; *Protecting Forests*; *Protecting Wildlife*; *Renewing Energy*; *Saving Water* (Chelsea House, 2003–04).

Desonie, Dana. *Humans and the Natural Environment* (Chelsea House, 2008).

Few, Roger. *Animal Watch* (DK, 2002).

Gallant, R.A. *Wonders of Biodiversity* (Benchmark, 2003).

Haddock, Patricia. *Environmental Time Bomb: Our Threatened Planet* (Enslow, 2000).

Mongillo, John, and Mongillo, Peter. *Teen Guides to Environmental Science*, 5 vols. (Greenwood, 2004).

Parker, Janice. *The Disappearing Forests* (Smart Apple Media, 2003).

Patent, D.H. *Biodiversity* (Clarion, 1996).

Penny, Malcolm. *Endangered Species: Our Impact on the Planet* (Raintree Steck-Vaughn, 2002).

Royston, Angela. *Energy of the Future* (Heinemann, 2007).

Saunders, Nigel, and Chapman, Steven. *Energy Essentials: Renewable Energy* (Raintree, 2004).

West, Krista, ed. *Critical Perspectives on Environmental Protection* (Rosen, 2007).

Index

I

L

M

N

O

P

R

S

T

U

W